LOST

IN THE MOUNTAINS OF DEATH

TRACEY TURNER

Crabtree Publishing Company
www.crabtreebooks.com

Crabtree Publishing Company
www.crabtreebooks.com
1-800-387-7650

616 Welland Ave.
St. Catharines, ON
L2M 5V6

PMB 59051, 350 Fifth Ave.
59th Floor,
New York, NY

Published by Crabtree Publishing Company in 2015.

Author: Tracey Turner

Illustrator: Nelson Evergreen

Project coordinator: Kelly Spence

Editor: Alex Van Tol, Kathy Middleton

Proofreader: Wendy Scavuzzo

Prepress technician: Ken Wright

Print and Production coordinator:
Katherine Berti

Text copyright © 2014 Tracey Turner

Illustration copyright © 2014 Nelson Evergreen

Copyright © 2014 A & C Black

Additional images © Shutterstock

First published 2014 by A & C Black, an imprint of Bloomsbury Publishing Plc.

WARNING!
The instructions in this book are for extreme survival situations only. Always proceed with caution, and ask an adult to supervise—or, if possible, seek expert help. If in doubt, consult a responsible adult.

Printed in Canada/102014/EF20140925

**Library and Archives Canada
Cataloguing in Publication**

Turner, Tracey, author
        Lost in the mountains of death / Tracey Turner.

(Lost : can you survive?)
Includes index.
ISBN 978-0-7787-0729-5 (bound).--
ISBN 978-0-7787-0737-0 (pbk.)

        1. Plot-your-own stories. I. Title.

PZ7.T883Lost 2014   j823'.92
C2014-904025-3

**Library of Congress
Cataloging-in-Publication Data**

Turner, Tracey.
  Lost in the Mountains of Death / by Tracey Turner ; illustration, Nelson Evergreen. -- American edition.
     pages cm. -- (Lost: can you survive?)
  ISBN 978-0-7787-0729-5 (reinforced library binding) -- ISBN 978-0-7787-0737-0 (pbk.)
  1. Plot-your-own stories. [1. Survival--Fiction. 2. Andes--Fiction. 3. Patagonia (Argentina and Chile)--Fiction. 4. Plot-your-own stories.] I. Evergreen, Nelson, 1971- illustrator. II. Title.

  PZ7.T8585Lq 2014
  [Fic]--dc23
                                        2014030525

Contents

South America

Caracas ★ ★ Port-of-Spain

VENEZUELA

Georgetown ★

★ Bogota

COLOMBIA

GUYANA

Paramaribo ★

SURINAME **FRENCH GUIANA**

Cayenne ★

ATLANTIC OCEAN

Quito ★

ECUADOR

PERU

Lima ★

T h e   A n d e s   M o u n t a i n s

★ La Paz

BRAZIL

Brasilia ★

BOLIVIA

The Atacama Desert

PARAGUAY

Asuncion ★

PACIFIC OCEAN

CHILE

Santiago ★

URUGUAY

Buenos Aires ★ Montevideo ★

ARGENTINA

SOUTH ATLANTIC OCEAN

PATAGONIA

★ Stanley

FALKLAND ISLANDS

Tierra del Fuego

Welcome to your adventure!
STOP! Read this first!

Welcome to an action-packed adventure in which you take the starring role!

You're about to enter the Patagonian Andes—a dizzying landscape of tall mountains, icy glaciers, and howling winds. Choose from different options on each page, according to your instincts, knowledge, and intelligence, and make your own path through the mountains to safety.

You decide:
- How to escape an attacking puma
- How to survive an avalanche
- How to avoid disaster on glaciers and frozen lakes

. . . and many more life-or-death dilemmas. Along the way, you'll discover the facts you need to help you survive.

It's time to test your survival skills—or die trying!

Your adventure starts on page 7.

Something ice cold splashes onto your face and you wake up with a start. You blink water from your eyes, sit up, and look out across a sparkling mountain landscape covered in freshly fallen snow. You're lying between some rocks with your backpack covering you. It's cold, but you're wearing warm layers.

It takes you a moment to remember where you are and what has happened. You were trekking with friends in the Andes, South America's spectacular mountain range, when an unseasonal snowstorm blew up and you were separated from the rest of your group. You look at your watch. It's eleven o'clock. The storm blew up hours ago! You must have banged your head and passed out. You're lucky to be alive.

You stand up and shout for your friends. Your voice echoes around the tall peaks that surround you. You strain your ears for a reply, but there isn't one. You try again, anyway. Nothing, except the drip of melting snow. High above you in the clear blue sky, a condor circles. You are completely lost—and entirely alone.

In your backpack, you have a number of useful things: crampons (to attach to your shoes so you can walk on ice), two thermal foil blankets, a container for boiling water, matches in a waterproof container, a couple of spare thermal T-shirts, a Swiss Army knife, a trowel, and a flashlight. You hoist your backpack onto your back and with no other option set off into the mountains.

How will you survive?

Turn to page 8 to find information you need to help you survive.

The Andes are the longest mountain range in the world, stretching more than 4,500 miles (7,000 km) along the western coast of South America. They stretch from the tropical rainforest in Venezuela, on the northern coast of South America, to the southernmost tip of Chile. The Andes are the highest mountains in the world outside of Asia. They're a vast and inhospitable environment, and many people have become lost in the Andes, never to return. If you're going to survive, you'll need to have your wits about you.

Patagonian Andes

You are in the Patagonian Andes, an area of about 386,000 square miles (1 million sq km) of spectacular scenery with high mountains, glaciers, and sparkling lakes. You came at the very beginning of the trekking season, which runs from November to April. This is summer in the southern hemisphere. But the weather here can be unpredictable and changeable, and you've been unlucky. Patagonia is a region, not a country, at the southern tip of South America, shared by the countries of Chile and Argentina.

Perils of the Andes

The temperature is one of the perils you will have to contend with, along with cold winds and the possibility of more snowstorms. Other dangers in the mountains are pumas, altitude sickness, steep drops, difficult terrain, avalanches, and earthquakes, which are common to this area.

Extreme Andes

The Andes span seven countries: Venezuela, Colombia, Ecuador, Peru, Bolivia, Chile, and Argentina. Because the Andes cover such a long distance, and the mountains are so high, the Andes mountain range is a land of extremes.

• The cloud forests of the Andes are found in the tropical north, where the warm air of the rainforest meets the cold air high in the mountains. Clouds form at the treetops.

• The Atacama Desert, in northern Chile, is one of the driest places on Earth. It is the highest desert in the world.

• The Andes are on the Pacific Ring of Fire (see page 37), where tectonic plates meet, often creating earthquakes, volcanoes, hot springs, and geysers.

• There are hundreds of thermal springs in the Andes caused by volcanic activity. El Tatio is a geyser field high up in the Andes with more than 80 active geysers. It's the largest geyser field in the southern hemisphere.

• The Tierra del Fuego archipelago is made up of one large island and lots of smaller ones. It is the world's most southern place where people live permanently. (People visit and stay in Antarctica, but they don't live there all the time.)

Turn to page 10.

Mountain Survival Tips

Here are a few basic tips that might affect your chances of survival in the mountains.

- The right clothes are vitally important in cold weather. Wear layers of clothing: the layer next to your skin should be able to keep moisture away from your body, the next layer should be warm, and the outer layer should be wind- and waterproof. Fortunately, you are warmly dressed, and you're wearing a hat, gloves, and sturdy walking boots.

- Make sure you know how to start a fire and make sure you practice before you set out on a trip somewhere cold. It could save your life. (Find out more about fire building on page 87.)

- If you get wet, take off your clothes and dry them and yourself before putting them back on. The water will make your body temperature drop very quickly and, even if the temperature seems quite mild, you'll be in danger of hypothermia.

- Don't try to climb steep inclines without the proper equipment and expertise.

- Making a shelter should be a priority when you're not walking. (Look at pages 15 and 71 for more on shelter building.)

Turn to page 11.

You've been walking some time when huge, gray clouds come racing over the tops of the mountains. They block the sun, and soon there's no sign of the blue sky anymore. As the air turns colder, your heart sinks—another storm must be on the way. Should you set off in the hope of finding your friends? Or should you stop and make a shelter?

If you decide to walk, go to page 24.

If you decide to make a shelter, go to page 14.

It gets more difficult to walk, until each step takes a huge effort. It doesn't look like it, but perhaps the slope is steeper here. Your head is still pounding. In fact, it seems to be getting worse, and you're starting to feel sick as well.

You think you've probably caught some kind of bug. Perhaps the best thing to do is find somewhere to stop and rest. Or maybe it would be better to head for lower ground.

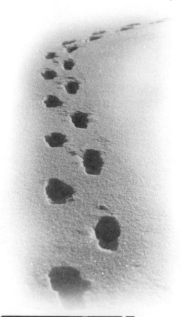

If you decide to find somewhere to rest, go to page 22.

If you decide to change direction and head for lower ground, go to page 44.

Slowly and carefully, you walk toward the rocks where you thought you saw movement. As you round a large boulder, you find out what it was. You are staring into the yellow eyes of a large puma.

You feel sweat break out on your forehead and you swallow hard. The animal is big and muscular. It hasn't taken its eyes off you, and its ears are flattened against its head. You figure that this probably isn't a good sign. In fact, it's difficult to see anything good about this situation. The puma is only a short distance away from you. Just a couple of large bounds on its powerful legs and it would be on top of you.

What should you do?

If you decide to curl into a ball and play dead, go to page 38.

If you decide to back off, go to page 27.

The clouds look as though they could burst with snow at any moment, and the wind howls around you in icy gusts. You look around for something to help make a shelter with before the storm arrives.

There are some rocks and boulders that you could shelter behind, using your blankets as covering, which would make a very quick shelter. There's also a small forest a bit farther down the slope where you could shelter in the trees.

If you opt for a quick shelter in the rocks, go to page 45.

If you choose to head for the trees, go to page 35.

Shelter Building

Which type of shelter you build depends on the conditions, how much time you have to build it (if it's getting dark, you'll have to be quick), how cold it is, or if there are dangerous wild animals around. Here are some general tips.

- If you're on high ground, head for somewhere lower down so that you're not so exposed to the wind. However, very low ground might be vulnerable to flooding, frost, and mist, so avoid that as well.

- Forest shelters are fairly easy to make and the tree canopy will also provide shelter from the elements. But be careful of falling branches.

- If there's a thunderstorm, beware of sheltering under trees, which may attract lightning.

- Even a shallow depression in the ground will give you some protection. If it's raining, it will soon turn into a muddy puddle. If you're on a flat plain and a storm blows up, your only choice might be to sit with your back to the wind and pile your equipment around you.

- More permanent shelters can be made by forming walls from logs or stones piled between two parallel rows of upright sticks. But be very careful with stones, they could collapse. But you'll need plenty of time to make a more sophisticated shelter like this one.

The storm is getting worse and the snow stings your face as the wind hurls around the strong, icy flurries. You're starting to shiver, and you're sure finding shelter is the right thing to do. But you don't know how long the storm is going to last and how long you'll be stuck here. Which type of shelter should you build?

You could simply find a spot sheltered by rocks and use your backpack and blankets as extra cover. This will only take a few moments.

Or you could construct a better shelter by finding a big boulder and digging out a trench behind it on the side facing away from the wind. Then you could build another wall around you out of large stones and snuggle down in the trench with your backpack and blankets over you.

If you decide to make a very basic shelter in the rocks, go to page 45.

If you decide to find a boulder and start digging a trench, go to page 26.

You know that the most important thing is to stop the bleeding, so you grab a spare T-shirt from your backpack and press it to the wound. After a few moments, the blood stops flowing. You tear the T-shirt into strips and make a bandage. You tie it firmly, but not too tightly, around your wound.

You sit down on a rock, have a drink of water, and feel much better. Something catches your eye. In the distance are some yellowy-white blobs, and you eventually realize that they're sheep. You can just about make out the fence keeping them in. A sheep farm must mean farmers!

You set off toward the fence.

Go to page 114.

The next part is a bit steep, and it's extremely windy up here. But you're determined to get to the next ridge. You'll have a condor's-eye view from there, and it's not very far away.

You remember that you should have both hands and one foot secure before you move the other foot, and you make sure that your hand-holds and the foot-hold for your left foot all feel comfortable and safe. You look down to see where the next foot-hold is for your right foot, and swing your leg up to get to it. But as you do so, your left foot slips, and you lose your hand-holds, too. Panic-stricken, you scramble desperately for another firm grip, but it's no good. You plummet downward, knocking your head as you fall.

The end.

Mountain Climbing

- You should never attempt to climb a mountain without proper gear (see below), training, experience, and expert knowledge. No wonder you fell! You shouldn't climb alone, either—you need other climbers for backup and safety.

- As well as all of the above, you'll need to make quick decisions and judgments that could mean the difference between life and death. So make sure you are alert and calm, have a clear head, and aren't in danger of panicking.

- You need to be fit and strong. Climbing mountains is physically demanding.

- Essential mountain-climbing gear includes a climbing helmet, ropes, harness, carabiners (which connect ropes together safely), ice ax, ice hammer, and climbing boots.

You were sure the blizzard would have blown over by now, but it's still howling around your ears and battering you with tiny icy snowflakes. You are shivering violently and you're very tired. You decide to sit down and wait out the storm.

The snow makes it difficult to see, and you feel very confused. Was it really just today you were walking with your friends? You struggle to remember. As you stagger over to a boulder and sit down, you realize you've stopped shivering. You feel exhausted but, strangely, you feel quite warm now and unzip your jacket. You slump sideways and fall asleep.

You have severe hypothermia. Unfortunately, you don't wake up.

The end.

Hypothermia

Doctors divide hypothermia into three phases:

- If your body temperature has fallen to between 89 and 95 degrees Fahrenheit (32 and 35 degrees Celsius), you have mild hypothermia. Symptoms include shivering, tiredness, and rapid breathing.

- You develop moderate hypothermia if your body temperature drops to 82 to 89°F (28 to 32°C). Symptoms include confusion and irrational behavior, difficulty moving, shallow breathing, and slurred speech. You will probably stop shivering—but this is definitely not a good sign.

- You have severe hypothermia when your body temperature is below 82°F (28°C). Your pulse becomes weak, your pupils dilate, or get large, and you will probably pass out. Even with medical attention, people in this stage of hypothermia might die. Without it, they certainly will.

You're feeling worse than before, and now you have a nasty cough as well. Maybe you'll feel better after a rest.

You sit down protected from the wind by some rocks. You take everything out of your backpack, put the blankets around your shoulders, and lay everything else out around you in a semicircle. Somewhere at the back of your mind you know this is an odd thing to do, but you decide not to worry about it.

Resting isn't going to make any difference to what's wrong with you. You have altitude sickness, and there's only one cure for it: descending to lower ground. If you don't, symptoms could get worse, and you could end up with swelling in your brain or a build-up of fluid in your lungs, both of which can be fatal. As you sit and rest, your symptoms become worse. You start to hallucinate before falling into a coma. You're dead within 24 hours.

The end.

Altitude Sickness

- People react to high altitudes differently. You were unlucky to experience altitude sickness, which can be treated by descending to lower ground. It's quite rare for altitude sickness to develop into high altitude cerebral edema (a buildup of fluid around the brain), or high altitude pulmonary edema (a buildup of fluid in the lungs). But when it does, it's often fatal.

- Early warning symptoms of altitude sickness are a headache, tiredness, and nausea. If you don't descend to lower ground, these symptoms will become worse, your heart might start to pound, and you might feel dizzy.

- Severe symptoms include breathlessness and coughing. People sometimes become very clumsy, and behave irrationally—which definitely isn't helpful when you're halfway up a mountain.

Even without the sun and blue sky, the landscape is beautiful. If you weren't lost and alone, you'd be enjoying the trek and the scenery. You're surrounded by snow-capped mountains and, here and there in the distance, you can see lakes and smooth, blue–white glaciers.

The clouds continue to roll over the mountaintops as you walk, and the wind gets stronger.

Go to page 42.

Andes Climate

- The Andes stretch all the way from the top of South America to the bottom, so the climate varies tremendously. In the north, the climate is tropical. But the Andes are so high, that they are still cold. Almost all of the world's tropical glaciers are found in the Andes. The southern part of the mountain range is much colder.

- The Andes Mountains are a barrier between the Pacific Ocean and the South American continent. To the west of the central Andes, the climate is very dry, and the eastern plains of Argentina also have extremely dry weather.

- You are in the Patagonian Andes down in the southern part of the continent, between Chile and Argentina. The weather is famously changeable here, and sudden storms are common, as you have found out.

You start digging with your trowel. The ground is very hard, but you're determined and finally succeed in making a shallow depression just about big enough to lie down in. The wind is stronger now, and the snow finds its way inside your jacket, making you wet as well as cold. You're chilled to the bone.

You're shivering, so you open your backpack to pull out a blanket, but it's instantly whipped out of your hand by the wind, and goes flying off into the distance. You take out the other blanket and wrap that around your shoulders. Teeth chattering, and feeling weak and exhausted, you go and sit down behind the boulder, abandoning your plans to make a shelter.

You are in the early stages of hypothermia. The blanket isn't enough to warm you up in this blizzard, especially since your clothes are damp. Soon, you fall unconscious.

The end.

You inch backward slowly, keeping your movements calm and controlled even though your heart is pounding wildly. The big cat is still staring in your direction, but it no longer seems ready to spring.

You step back farther and keep still. The puma flicks its ears, then turns and bounds away, moving fast. You breathe a long sigh of relief as you watch it. Soon the animal is out of sight.

Go to page 30.

You don't have much farther to go before you find it: a fast-flowing stream, which must be fed by meltwater from the mountain.

You are pretty sure that this water will be safe to drink, but you make a fire (see page 87 for more on making fires) and boil it anyway. You're already lost, and you don't want to risk getting sick as well.

You drink some of the water once it's cooled a bit, and the hot drink—even though it's just water—makes you feel a bit better. The crackling fire is good for your spirits, too. Once you've filled your water bottle, you put out the fire carefully.

Go to page 58.

Water Needs

- Even in cold weather, you still need to drink over two pints (1 L) of water per day to replace what you lose by breathing and sweating—more if you're doing hard work. If you don't drink enough, you're in danger of dehydration, which can kill you. Luckily, there's plenty of water in the Andes.

- It's always a good idea to boil water before drinking it, even if it's from a clear mountain stream like this one. There could be a dead animal in the water farther upstream out of sight.

- You could also melt ice or snow to drink. But don't eat snow without melting it first—if you're already cold, eating snow will make you even colder. And don't eat crushed ice, because it could injure your mouth.

The sun has come out, and the tall peaks of the Andes look even more dramatic against the blue sky. But you're feeling jumpy and too nervous to enjoy the scenery. You realize there are many dangers in this remote part of the world.

Maybe you should stay here where it seems relatively safe, rather than risk rockfalls, avalanches, steep drops, and dangerous wildlife if you keep traveling.

If you decide to keep going, go to page 74.

If you decide to stay put and await rescue, go to page 98.

You scramble up the mountainside, scattering small rocks as you go. It's steeper and more difficult than it looked. You don't have any climbing gear, but you're not planning to climb up vertical cliffs. Even so, perhaps you should find an easier route.

If you decide to climb back down and find a less difficult path, go to page 46.

If you decide to continue climbing, go to page 18.

The ground shakes beneath your feet again. You squat down, and an even more violent tremor almost makes you lose your balance. You're very glad you're not near anything that could topple down on you, such as the rocks and boulders from the mountainside.

Earthquakes are not uncommon here: the Andes are on the Pacific Ring of Fire, where the tectonic plates that make up Earth's crust meet and collide with one another (for more on earthquakes, go to page 37).

The ground stops shaking. You're aware that there could be another quake at any time, but you can't stay here forever. You need to keep moving. A quick movement catches your eye. Scuttling away from the mountainside is a small grey furry shape—a chinchilla. Maybe it was disturbed by the tremor.

Watching the animal scurry into the distance, you take out your water bottle, but it's empty. You're thirsty, and look around for a water source. There's snow higher up on the mountain. You could make a fire and melt some. Or you could go in search of a stream.

If you decide to melt snow, go to page 50.

If you decide to find a stream, go to page 89.

Chinchillas

- You were lucky to see a chinchilla. They're rare animals in the wild, and they're usually active at dawn and dusk.

- Chinchillas can measure up to about 12 inches (30 cm) long. In the wild, they live only in the Andes in Peru and Chile in groups of up to 100 animals.

- Eagles, pumas, and foxes prey on chinchillas. Chinchillas use a clever trick—they can shed a clump of fur if they are grabbed by a predator, allowing them to get away unharmed.

- They are very agile and can jump up to six feet (1.8 m) high.

- Chinchillas are rare partly because of their very soft, warm coats. They have been hunted for their fur.

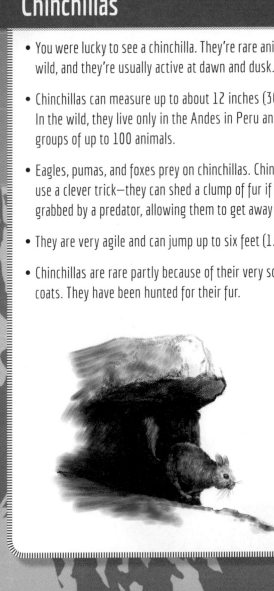

The clouds roll away across the mountains and the sun shines on the fresh snow. It's starting to melt already.

You're distracted from the spectacular view by a terrible headache. You feel tired, too, even though you've just had a rest. You're feeling a bit sick as well.

This would be a terrible time to get sick. But you don't feel that bad, you tell yourself. Maybe you should just keep going and hope you feel better soon. On the other hand, you've heard that being high up can make you sick. Perhaps you should head for lower ground.

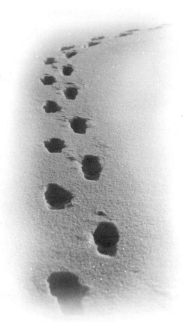

If you decide to head for lower ground, go to page 44.

If you decide to keep going as you are, go to page 12.

You shelter under a bent tree. After an hour or so, the wind starts to die down. Soon the snow stops, and the air feels a little warmer. You crawl out from underneath the tree and make your way to the edge of the woods.

You look out across a wide valley, beautiful in the fresh snow. You can see quite a long way, but there are no signs of life. Optimistically, you call out for your friends again, but all you hear in reply is the echo of your own voice.

You wonder if you should climb up higher. Perhaps with a good view, you'll be able to spot the rest of your group.

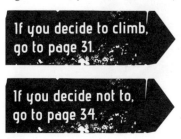

If you decide to climb, go to page 31.

If you decide not to, go to page 34.

The ground trembles again, this time more strongly, and small stones come skittering down the rocks.

You're beginning to wonder whether you should have taken cover, when the ground suddenly rocks violently, knocking you off your feet. You hit the ground hard and, as you struggle to get up, the sound of crashing and tumbling makes you look up. Huge boulders dislodged by the earthquake are crashing down the mountainside. Unfortunately, you are right in their path, and there's nothing you can do to get out of the way.

The end.

Earthquakes

- Earth's crust is made up of enormous tectonic plates, that move and grind against one another constantly. When two plates grind together, and one slips, it causes an earthquake.

- The border between the Pacific Plate and other large tectonic plates lies around the edge of the Pacific Ocean. An arc that these plates make around the Pacific Ocean is known as the Pacific Ring of Fire. It stretches from New Zealand, through New Guinea, the Philippines, and Japan, and across the Pacific Ocean to the western coasts of North and South America. Not surprisingly, earthquakes are very common in this area.

- Most of the world's earthquakes are very minor. But big ones can cause large numbers of casualties and terrible damage when buildings topple and cracks open up in Earth's crust.

- Millions of years ago, the colliding tectonic plates of the Pacific Ring of Fire caused the Andes Mountains to form.

- Volcanoes are also common around the Pacific Ring of Fire. Seventy five percent of the world's volcanoes, both active and dormant, are found here. The highest volcanoes in the world are in the Andes. The highest is Ojos del Salado on the Chile-Argentina border, which is about 22,600 feet (6,900 m) high.

You have made a fatal mistake. Pumas are opportunistic predators and, if they see the chance of an easy kill, they will take it. When you were standing up, the puma was probably just as worried about you as you were about it. But now that you've curled up into a ball, defenseless and vulnerable, it sees you as easy prey.

The animal is powerful and fast. It's only a matter of seconds before it's all over.

The end.

Pumas

- Pumas are also known as mountain lions, cougars, and catamounts. They're very shy, solitary animals, so they're rarely seen.

- These animals are large and powerful. They weigh an average of up to about 130 pounds (59 kg) and can weigh up to 200 pounds (92 kg). Their head and body measure up to about five feet (1.5 m), plus an extra 27 inches (69 cm) or so for the tail.

- Pumas are found in North and South America, from Canada down to the Andes in southern Chile. They once roamed the entire United States, but now they're only found on the west coast and in Florida. The endangered Florida panther is a type of puma, despite its name.

- These big cats prey on animals as large as deer and vicuñas. In this part of the Andes, they also prey on guanacos and south Andean deer, as well as smaller prey such as hares. They usually kill by delivering a fatal bite to the back of the neck, so at least it's over quickly for you.

- If they've made a big kill, pumas will keep it hidden and return to it over a few days.

- Pumas have been known to attack people, usually a person out hiking on their own. But human attacks are rare.

It gets darker as the night draws in, and you turn on your flashlight. The tiny patch of ground it lights up only makes you feel more vulnerable. It's cold, too—you can't move fast enough to keep yourself warm because of the darkness. You're beginning to wish you'd stopped to build a shelter, but it's going to be tricky to do that in the darkness.

Just as you decide to stop and find somewhere to sleep for the night, you slip and plummet down a steep slope you hadn't realized was there. In a few seconds, it's all over.

The end.

The Andes' Highest Peaks

- The Andes mountain range is second only to the Himalayas (and its associated ranges) for the world's highest mountains.

- Aconcagua in Argentina is the highest mountain in the Andes at 21,955 feet (6,962 m).

- The second highest, Ojos del Salado, is also the highest active volcano in the world, although it hasn't erupted since around 700 CE. It's on the border between Chile and Argentina, overlooking the Atacama Desert, which is one of the driest places on Earth.

- Although Aconcagua is the highest peak, it's not the most difficult to climb. Mount Fitzroy (also known as Cerro Chaltén), in the Patagonian Andes in Chile, is only 11,072 feet (3,375 m), less than half as high as Aconcagua, yet it is a notoriously hard climb because of its sheer rock face. Only very experienced climbers attempt it.

- Chimborazo is the highest mountain in Ecuador at 20,564 feet (6,268 m) and lies on the equator. Even though there are taller mountains, its peak is the farthest point on Earth's surface from the center of Earth. This is because of the equatorial bulge. There's a bulge of 26.54 miles (42.71 km) at the equator, caused by Earth's rotation.

The wind bites viciously, and the snow stings your face. Maybe it would be better to stop and find some kind of shelter—if you can in these conditions.

If you decide to stop and find shelter, go to page 16.

If you decide to brave the blizzard, go to page 20.

You fit into the cave quite snugly. You take out your thermal blankets and wrap them around you. Protected from the wind, you feel much warmer.

The sun has nearly set, and it's getting colder. It would be lovely to have a fire to keep you warm and perhaps make a hot drink. But would it be worth the effort?

If you decide to make a fire, go to page 86.

If you decide not to bother and go to sleep in your shelter, go to page 80.

You do start to feel better now that you're on lower ground. It's easier to breathe, and you don't feel so tired or sick. You were experiencing mild altitude sickness, which affects some people at higher altitudes and can develop into a life-threatening condition if you don't descend to lower ground. (Find out more about altitude sickness on page 23.)

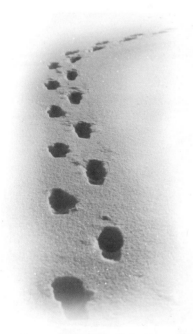

You think you spot movement in the rocks ahead of you— something big. Should you go and investigate, or should you stay away in case it's a dangerous animal?

If you decide to investigate the movement, go to page 13.

If you decide to walk in a different direction, go to page 30.

Your shelter is very basic, but it protects you from the snow and the extremely fierce wind. All you have to do now is stay as warm as you can under your blankets and wait out the blizzard.

It's not long before the wind stops howling and things sound much calmer. After a little longer, you're sure the storm is over, and you stick your head outside. The clouds are moving swiftly away, and you can make out a watery sun behind them.

Go to page 34.

You scramble back down the rocks. Looking up, you can see it was too difficult a climb to attempt without proper climbing gear, and you probably wouldn't be able to see your friends anyway if they can't hear you when you shout. You shout again, just in case. There's still no reply.

You walk along flatter ground. You feel fine, aside from a nagging headache.

Go to page 34.

You were taking a bit of a chance by heading for the trees. But luckily it doesn't take long to reach them, and there's still some light left. One of them is a huge conifer, and its branches reach all the way to the ground. You peer inside—it's like a ready-made tent. You're protected from the wind and you even have a soft carpet of pine needles to sleep on.

It would be lovely to have a fire to keep you warm, and perhaps make a hot drink. But is it worth the effort?

If you decide to make a fire, go to page 86.

If you decide not to bother and go to sleep in your shelter, go to page 80.

You step onto the snow with a crunch. It seems pretty easy to walk on, and the wind does seem a bit less fierce this way. As you trudge across the slope, you hear a "thunking" sound. You wonder what it could be. Maybe there's someone walking higher up. You call out.

The "thunking" sound is followed by a rumble, then cracks appear in the snow. You freeze, then turn and make a run for it. But you're too late. The snow cracks up and starts to slide downhill, taking you with it. You're hurtled downhill and buried under a thick layer of snow, which sets rock-hard within moments.

The end.

Avalanches

- There are usually warning signs that an avalanche is likely. In this case, the recent earthquake was a sign that you should stay away from areas where an avalanche could occur.

- After an avalanche, the snow sets as hard as cement within seconds, making it impossible to move or breathe. You won't be able to dig yourself out once the avalanche has stopped, unless you're very near the surface.

- There are two types of avalanches: a loose snow avalanche is made up of powdery snow, and isn't usually dangerous; a slab avalanche is when big chunks of heavy snow break away from a layer of snow underneath them, and is very dangerous. Snow in a slab avalanche can hurtle down a mountainside at 80 miles an hour (129 kph).

- If there's a heavy snowfall, the fresh snow can make the layer of snow underneath it unstable. Avalanche warnings are issued under these conditions.

- Most avalanches are caused by the weight of a skier, snowboarder, or snowmobile on snow that is unstable.

It's a bit of a climb up to where there's still snow on the mountain. You make your way carefully, choosing a path that allows you to walk upright, without needing to use your hands to climb. You realize that would be extremely dangerous, even though there's a much quicker route to where the snow is. You don't want to risk a fall, which you know would spell your doom.

It's cold and windy here, and you make a fire as quickly as you can in the shelter of some rocks (see page 87 for more on making a fire). You melt snow in your container, drink some, and melt more to fill your bottle. Then you carefully put out the fire and carry on.

Go to page 58.

Dangerous Mountains

Mountain climbing can be fun and exhilarating, but it can also be very dangerous. These are some of the world's most dangerous mountains to climb.

- Mont Blanc is in the Alps, on the border between France and Italy. It's popular with climbers, but has claimed thousands of lives.

- Only 191 people have tried to climb Annapurna in the Himalayas, which is more than 26,000 feet (8,000 m) high. Sixty-one of them have died trying.

- More than 700 people a year now reach the summit of Mount Everest, the world's tallest mountain at 29,029 feet (8,848 m). Hundreds have died in the attempt since the first person reached the summit in 1953.

- Mount Fitzroy in the Patagonian Andes is a difficult climb, because of its sheer granite faces. Its isolated location means that few people try to climb it—roughly one person per year.

You search in your backpack for something to make into a pair of gloves, or at least mittens, and you find an old thermal T-shirt.

Before you start, you make sure your bootlaces are securely tied. You rip the T-shirt in half and wind the material around one hand, making sure you can still move your fingers. Then you wrap an elastic band around it. It's trickier doing the same to the other hand, but you manage it with the help of your teeth. It's going to be difficult tying your shoelaces from now on, but at least your hands are warm.

Go to page 76.

The dawn light wakes you up and you peer out of your shelter. You're still completely lost and have absolutely no idea which direction is best. You look at the landscape to decide which way to go. You could either climb a gentle slope and walk along higher ground, or go down a slightly steeper slope to lower ground.

If you decide to head for higher ground, go to page 72.

If you decide walking on lower ground would be better, go to page 64.

There's a roaring noise behind you. You spin around, and suddenly you're very glad that you moved away from the snow—it's rushing down the mountain in an avalanche. You stand and watch for a while, until the snow stops moving and silence descends again. The snow has built up into a huge drift: if you were buried underneath it, the chances of getting out alive seem slim. Thank goodness you decided not to walk across the snow.

The sun's beginning to go down. Soon it will be twilight. Maybe you should build a shelter for the night.

If you decide to build a shelter, go to page 70.

If you decide to carry on, go to page 40.

Surviving an Avalanche

- If you're going skiing or snowboarding, always check for avalanche warnings before you leave. If you can't get avalanche reports, don't head for the slopes after a heavy snowfall (which could destabilize the snow underneath it), or if there have been earthquakes.

- If you're caught in an avalanche, try to keep hold of a ski pole, if you have one. You can poke it out of the snow to alert rescuers, as long as you're near enough to the surface.

- Take off your skis, they'll only make things worse.

- Always carry a transceiver, which will tell rescuers where you are.

- As the avalanche draws to a stop, try to make an air space in front of your face by vigorously punching at the snow. It will set hard very quickly.

- Don't shout out unless you're sure rescuers are close by, otherwise you'll be wasting precious air.

You shoo the birds away, take some of the meat and make a small fire (see page 87). You use a sharp stick to act as a spit, reasoning that the heat will kill any bacteria that might be present. When it's cooked, you dig in hungrily.

But you soon bitterly regret having eaten the meat. As you continue on your way, you start to feel pains in your stomach. An hour or so later, you begin to vomit. Then the diarrhea starts . . . things are not looking good.

You retch violently, feeling weak and sick. You know that without a supply of clean water to replace the fluids you're losing, you'll dehydrate. You dig the blankets out of your backpack and slump against a rock. You don't have the energy to make a proper shelter. As night draws in, you die of hypothermia (see page 21).

The end.

Food Poisoning

- Food poisoning can be caused by bacteria (which is what happened in this case, since the meat wasn't freshly killed), or a virus. It causes vomiting and diarrhea and can last for several days.

- Food poisoning can be caused by not cooking or storing food properly, or food can become contaminated from a person touching it with dirty hands or an animal touching it with dirty paws, claws, or beaks.

- Foods that are especially likely to cause food poisoning are raw meat, eggs, shellfish, and ready-prepared foods such as sandwiches.

- Symptoms of food poisoning usually start a day or so after eating the contaminated food, but some types can make the victim ill almost right away. In these cases, vomiting is the main symptom.

- Usually, victims of food poisoning don't need medical attention. As long as they drink plenty of water and get rest, they recover.

- Without drinking water, the victim can become dehydrated, which is potentially fatal.

Ahead of you stretches a flat, white, sloping plain of thick snow. Maybe the blizzard was worse here, or perhaps the snow has never melted here. It lies in the shadow of the mountain that towers above you, pointing craggy peaks into the brilliant blue sky. Maybe you should walk across the snow? Your boots are waterproof, and it looks as though it's easy going.

If you decide to change direction and head away from the snow, go to page 54.

If you decide to trudge across the snowy slope, go to page 48.

You run to the stream. The blood is pouring from your wounded hand, and you're feeling the energy draining out of your body as it flows.

You plunge your hand into the stream. It's ice cold, which only makes the blood flow more freely, and it chills you to the bone. To make matters worse, you get your clothes wet in your rush to put your hand in the water. Your teeth start to chatter.

Feeling weak from blood loss, you slump down next to a tree by the stream. The bleeding begins to lessen but, with no one around to help you, your body temperature drops until you become hypothermic and die.

The end.

You trudge along, feeling very tired. At least your improvised gloves are keeping your hands warm.

Snow-capped mountains soar above you, and the sun is out. But you're finding it very difficult to keep your spirits up. The mountains only remind you of how vast and remote this landscape is and how small you are.

Go to page 112.

From your high vantage point, the landscape sweeps down into wooded valleys. Sunlight glints on a distant lake. Snowy mountain peaks stretch into the distance.

You're finding it difficult to appreciate the lovely scenery, though, because of a thumping headache. You're a bit out of breath, too, maybe because you're traveling uphill. Perhaps you should travel on lower ground.

If you decide to keep going on uphill, go to page 79.

If you decide to turn back and travel on lower ground, go to page 64.

You can see the blue lake glittering below you, and you're still wondering whether it might make a better route. But, just then, there's a scuffling sound above you that makes you look up. On the rocks, just out of reach above your head, is a small furry animal. It's a guinea pig!

You know that it's common to eat guinea pigs in this part of the world. In fact, people breed them for eating. You're feeling very hungry. Maybe you should go after the guinea pig, and catch and roast it. After all, you won't get very far if you become too weak.

If you decide to go after the animal, go to page 108.

If you decide to keep going, go to page 96.

You cautiously you put one foot onto the ice, pressing down to make sure it doesn't crack or move. It seems to be safe, and you let the ice take your full weight. The surface of the ice looks solid, and you can't hear any cracking sounds. Crossing the lake here will save you lots of time. You walk out onto the ice, taking careful, sliding steps.

It's not long, though, before the ice does start to crack. You try to race back the way you came, but you're too late. The ice breaks, and you plunge into the icy water. You don't have time to haul yourself out before hypothermia sets in. You struggle out of the ice-cold water and make it to the bank. But, by this time, you're too confused and disoriented to get warm and dry and save yourself.

The end.

There are two condors circling in the sky, getting lower and lower. One of them swoops down—it looks as though it landed just on the other side of a rocky outcrop. Slowly, so as not to alarm the bird, you step around the rocks. Only a short distance away from you, there are three of the large birds feasting on something. It looks as though it could be a dead guanaco. Another condor swoops down to join the others in their meal.

The birds are surprisingly ugly close up, with bald heads and hooked beaks. One of them spots you and gives an alarmed cry, hopping backward from the carrion, with its massive wings outstretched. The condor's wingspan looks twice your height! The bird cocks its head to look at you, then hops back to the dead animal.

Hunger gnaws at your stomach. Should you chase away the condors and eat some of the meat yourself?

If you decide to eat some of the meat, go to page 56.

If you decide to leave the condors to their feast, go to page 73.

Andean Condors

- Andean condors are some of the world's largest flying birds. They weigh up to about 33 pounds (15 kg) and have a huge wingspan of up to 10.5 feet (3.2 m). Although the wandering albatross has a wider wingspan, Andean condors' wings are the largest of any bird.

- Because they're so large, that wide wingspan needs a bit of help. The condors live in areas where there are high winds so they can surf air currents without having to flap their wings.

- Andean condors are black. The male birds have a white collar around their necks. They have bald heads, similar to other vultures.

- Like all vultures, condors feed mainly on carrion, though they sometimes raid other birds' nests for eggs or newly hatched chicks.

- Andean condors are endangered. There are only a few thousand of them left.

You've never walked on a glacier before, but it looks simple enough. You strap on your crampons and head out onto the ice. It's more difficult than you thought, and it takes you a while to get used to walking on the spikes of your crampons. You learn, after slipping, that you have to put your feet flat onto the surface of the ice. It's quite tiring.

You're getting the hang of it and making good progress when something catastrophic happens. The layer of snow you're walking on suddenly gives way and you tumble into a crevasse. You hit your head and die instantly.

The end.

Crevasses

- Crevasses are cracks in a glacier or ice sheet. They can be up to 22 yards (20 m) across, 150 feet (46 m) deep, and hundreds of feet (meters) long.

- Crevasses can be impossible to see under a bridge of snow, which may not be thick enough to take a person's weight. They can trick even the most experienced climbers.

- Because of the danger of crevasses, it's important for trekkers to rope themselves together. That way, if someone does fall into a crevasse, they can be pulled out by the rest of the group.

- Anyone planning to travel on a glacier should take special training in crevasse-rescue techniques.

- Glaciers are moving rivers of ice, so new crevasses open up all the time, and old ones close.

You hardly notice the dangerous drop and loose rocks surrounding you because you're so focused on your hunt. There it is again! A brownish, furry shape disappears into some rocks above you. There's a short climb to get to where it vanished, and you fearlessly haul yourself up, hand over hand, flailing around for footholds with your feet.

Once you've made the climb, though, you find yourself on a perilously narrow ledge. For the first time, you realize the seriousness of your predicament. You are perched on a thin ledge with a drop of about sixty-five feet (20 m) below you. There is no sign of the guinea pig. A gust of wind sweeps the ledge, nearly taking you with it.

You gulp and start to climb down. Climbing without the correct gear in a strong wind is, of course, highly dangerous. You climb down about three feet (1 m) before you slip and fall.

The end.

Guinea Pigs

- Guinea pigs are descended from wild rodents called cavies, which are slightly different—and one has just spelled your doom.

- The animals are native to South America where guinea pigs are bred for food. They breed easily and don't take up much space, so they're a very popular source of protein. Guinea pigs were first raised by humans around 3,000 years ago.

- In North America and Europe, guinea pigs are kept as pets. There is evidence that they were kept as pets as far back as the 1500s in Europe, after the Spanish conquistadors brought the animals back from the newly discovered New World.

- Cavies also have larger relatives. One of them is the capybara, the world's largest rodent. It looks like a giant guinea pig and is also from South America. Another is the mara, which looks more like a large hare or a jackrabbit.

In the gathering dusk, there isn't much time for building a shelter. You spot a small opening in the rocks close by, which might mean you won't have to bother. You take a closer look: it's a small, dark cave. It doesn't look very cozy, but it would offer protection from the wind.

Or maybe you should go in search of a different shelter. There are some trees in the distance, and you think it should only take you half an hour or so to reach them.

If you decide to shelter in the cave, go to page 43.

If you decide to walk to the trees, go to page 47.

Shelter

- Unless you're somewhere very hot and low on water, shelter should be your first priority in a survival situation. In very cold conditions, you won't last long without protection from the weather.

- Use whatever materials are at hand to make your shelter. On a snow-covered mountainside with no trees, it's possible to make a shelter by cutting snow into blocks. People who live in the Arctic all year round sometimes construct shelters from turf.

- Try not to get your clothing wet in very cold conditions. You might work up a sweat building a shelter so, before you start your hard work, take off the layer of clothing closest to your skin, leaving on a waterproof layer. Take off the waterproof layer when you've finished your hard work and can dry yourself off. Or wear a material that keeps moisture away from your body.

- Whatever type of shelter you have, make sure it has air vents. If it doesn't, you'll die.

- Wet clothes can be left outside your shelter overnight. They'll freeze, and in the morning, you can shake off the ice. Keep in mind that they might not be totally dry by morning.

The wind feels colder the higher you go, and the going is difficult. You huff and puff as you climb the steep slope. You begin to wish you'd done a bit more training before setting off on the trek.

Go to page 61.

You watch the condors for a bit longer before continuing on your way. You skirt around the birds so as not to disturb them. You're far enough away from them that they look up and watch you but don't leave their meal. One of them watches you for awhile with something long, red, and glossy hanging from its beak.

Go to page 88.

Y ou have a sudden strange sensation as you walk. It feels as though the ground is vibrating slightly. Above you, a few small stones come skittering down the mountainside. The last of the stones bounce down, and everything is quiet again.

It must have been a very minor earthquake. You remember hearing that the area is prone to them. Maybe, to be on the safe side, you should change direction and find somewhere to walk that isn't near possible falling rocks. On the other hand, it was a very small vibration, and the shaking has completely stopped now. It might be better to just carry on your way.

If you decide to find somewhere away from the mountainside, go to page 32.

If you decide to carry on as you are, go to page 36.

No matter how cold the temperature, it's always best to take off wet clothing and get dry.

You begin to shiver uncontrollably in your wet clothes, and your teeth start chattering. You sit down to rest on a rock, and notice that you've stopped shivering. Maybe this is a good sign. But then you start to feel confused. You look around you: how did you get here? Anyway, it doesn't matter because you feel very tired and decide to lie down and go to sleep.

You have hypothermia (see page 21 for more information), and never wake up.

The end.

You spot movement out of the corner of your eye. In the distance, you make out a group of eight small deer.

These are South Andean deer, which only live in this part of the world. They're rare, so you're lucky to see them.

The animals haven't caught sight of you. You must be downwind of them. They start to move off calmly, and you wonder if you should follow them. They might lead you to water, and you need to fill up your water bottle.

If you decide to follow the deer, go to page 83.

If you decide not to follow them, go to page 60.

South Andean Deer

- South Andean deer, or huemul, are the national symbol of Chile and appear on the Chilean coat of arms.

- The animals are about 31.5 inches (80 cm) tall and brown or brownish gray in color.

- They are only found in the Andes in southern Chile and Argentina.

- Their numbers have decreased dramatically in the last 100 years, and they're now in serious danger of becoming extinct.

- The deer are preyed on by pumas and foxes, but habitat loss is their greatest threat.

You put your hands under your armpits to keep them warm as you walk. But when you need to tie your bootlace, your fingers get very cold very quickly. Maybe you should stop now to try to make some gloves?

If you decide to make something to keep your hands warm, go to page 52.

If you decide to keep going as you are, go to page 84.

The wind whistles around your ears. Despite the fact that you're walking as fast as you can, you're absolutely freezing. Your headache is worse—a searing pain presses behind your eyes—and you're finding it even more difficult to breathe. Wearily, you sit down and drink some water. It takes an enormous effort to get up again.

You really should have turned back. You stop and rest, but don't get any farther. A mixture of altitude sickness (see page 23), exhaustion, and hypothermia (see page 21) combine to kill you.

The end.

You crawl into your shelter feeling extremely tired. Night falls, and you're quickly asleep.

During the night, the temperature drops as cooler air sweeps down from the mountains. Your body temperature drops so much that you develop hypothermia as you sleep. You wake up but when you do, you're too tired and confused to take any action. You go to sleep again, and this time you don't wake up.

The end.

Fire for Survival

- Fire is the most important element for survival in cold conditions. It keeps you warm, which is vital to keeping you alive in colder climates, and a fire cheers you up and makes you feel as though you are in control. This is an important factor for survival when you're lost and alone.

- A fire should create warmth that will continue for most of the night. Heated stones will continue to give off heat for hours.

- A fire means you can cook food and boil water to make it fit for drinking. It can also be used to dry damp clothes.

- You can use small stones from the fire to dry out boots. Drop them into your boots using two sticks. Hot sand can also be used. Shovel it up in a metal container, but check often to make sure the insides of the boots aren't burning.

- However, fires can also be extremely dangerous. Make sure you're not in danger of starting a forest fire, and that you can light it, contain it, and put it out again safely.

You're soaked from the knees down. You take off your wet pants, socks, and shoes, hopping from foot to foot to try to keep warm. At least you don't feel any colder without your wet clothes, but you're still absolutely freezing. You pull a spare T-shirt out of your backpack and rub your wet skin vigorously until you're dry. Then you wrap yourself up in a blanket and gather materials for a fire. This isn't easy with the blanket wrapped around the bottom of your legs and feet but luckily, you don't have to go far to find some bark for tinder, twigs for kindling, and bigger twigs for the fire. (See page 87 for how to make a fire.)

Once the fire is burning, you put your boots, socks, and pants out to dry, and take the opportunity to have a rest. You take two sturdy twigs, pick up some hot stones near the fire, and drop them into your boots to dry them out. You soon feel warm again. By the time your clothes and boots are dry, you're feeling fine.

Go to page 109.

By the time you arrive, the animals have moved on but you were right in thinking they might lead to water. You discover a small shallow pond where they had been grazing. Sunlight glints on the surface of the water. It looks clear and clean.

It would take time and energy to make a fire, and you're very thirsty. You know that the water in the Andes is famous for being pure and safe to drink. Also, you reason that the water must be clean if the animals drink it, so maybe it's not worth the bother of boiling it?

If you make a fire and drink boiled water, go to page 60.

If you decide to drink the water without boiling it, go to page 106.

You keep walking, warming your hands under your armpits as you go. You often need to use your hands to keep your balance or to tie a bootlace, and they start to get cold.

Eventually, when dusk begins to fall, you need to make a shelter and fire for the night. But, without gloves, your hands soon become numb. You succeed in putting a shelter together, but your hands are too shaky to make a fire. You manage to get to sleep, but your body temperature drops too much during the night. You become hypothermic and die.

The end.

Frostbite

- It's important to keep your hands warm. When you need to do something to help you survive, such as make a fire, numb hands will prevent you from doing it.

- In colder conditions, below 34°F (1°C), fingers and toes can be vulnerable to frostbite, or the freezing of skin and tissues.

- White or waxy-looking fingers, or tingling and numbness, can be early signs of frostbite. Fingers should be warmed up by placing them under your armpits or in warm, but not hot, water.

- Never rub frostbitten fingers or toes. This causes more damage.

- Very severe cases of frostbite need surgery or even amputation.

Luckily you've practiced lighting fires many times before your trip to the mountains, so you know how to do it safely and efficiently. You gather together some bark, small twigs, and logs. Your matches have survived undamaged and dry, and you light one on the first try, sheltering it from the wind. Soon you have a healthy fire going inside a ring of stones, which will give off heat later on when the fire's died down.

You hold out your hands to the fire, feeling pleased with yourself and optimistic about a good night's sleep tonight, and finding rescue tomorrow. You heat up some water over the fire and drink it hot, which makes you feel even warmer. You go to sleep snug and dry.

Go to page 53.

Making a Fire

- Before you start, gather together everything you'll need: matches, tinder, kindling, and fuel.

- Choose an area that's sheltered and dry.

- Light your tinder. Tinder is very dry, flammable material, such as powdered bark, cotton cloth or cotton balls, or the inside of a bird's nest. Good tinder will only need a spark to light it.

- Stand your kindling around the tinder in a pyramid. Kindling is small, dry twigs that will burn quickly and easily.

- Gradually add larger pieces of wood. Take care not to add anything too big or too wet in the early stages, or you'll put the fire out.

- If there are stones available, place them in a circle around your fire. The stones will heat up and give off warmth after the fire has gone out, and they'll also stop the fire from spreading out of control. But be careful not to use very wet stones—they can explode!

You nearly trip over one of your bootlaces. They have come undone on both boots. You take off your gloves to tie them, crouching down with your back against a sudden strong gust of wind.

When you're finished, you turn to pick up the gloves from the rock. But they're not where you left them. The wind must have blown them off the rock! You start searching. Unfortunately, you look just in time to see one of them flying off down a very steep slope—far too dangerous for you to follow. The other glove is lying on the ground not far away but, as you reach it, the wind catches the glove, and whirls it over the precipice after the first one.

Does it matter that you've lost the gloves? Should you spend time and energy figuring out how to make some new ones? The weather's cold, but these aren't Arctic conditions.

If you decide to try to make some new gloves, go to page 52.

If you decide not to bother, go to page 78.

You're really thirsty now, and you know there must be a stream around here somewhere—there's no shortage of water in the Andes. There's a lush green forest ahead of you, and you think you can hear the sound of running water, although the high, buffeting wind makes it difficult to tell.

You carry on, heading toward the source of the sound.

Go to page 28.

Your stomach growls again. But you decide it's better to be hungry than risk eating a plant you're not completely sure about, and you're not feeling too weak yet.

You sense you're being watched and you spin around. You have to squint to see it but, sitting on some rocks staring at you, is a gray animal that is well camouflaged against the rocks. It looks like a fox. You decide not to disturb it but, while you're looking at the fox, you're not watching where you're putting your feet. You stumble over a big stone, fall, and badly gash your hand on a sharp rock.

Blood is pouring from the deep wound. What should you do?

If you decide to bandage the wound, go to page 17.

If you decide to wash it in a nearby stream, go to page 59.

Patagonian Foxes

- The animal you've seen is a Patagonian fox, or South American gray fox, which is native to Patagonia and western Argentina.

- These small predators weigh up to about ten pounds (4.5 kg). They mostly prey on rodents. They also eat berries, birds' eggs, and insects, and scavenge carrion or pumas' leftovers.

- The foxes' favorite food is hares, which aren't native to Patagonia. They were introduced from Europe in the 1800s.

- Patagonian foxes help one another out. Female foxes that don't have cubs share their food with other female foxes and their cubs. This cooperative behavior helps the species survive.

You walk downhill across rocky terrain to the lake that is sparkling in the sunshine. Close to the shore, there's a beautiful sight: a flock of Chilean flamingos, bright pink against the blue water, feeding in the shallows.

Keeping your distance from the birds so as not to scare them off, you make a fire at the lake to boil water to fill your water bottle. The feeding birds remind you that the lake is probably full of food. The birds eat snails and aquatic insects, but there are bound to be fish here, too. Your stomach rumbles at the thought. Should you stop and fish? Some food would make you feel a lot better.

If you decide to fish in the lake, go to page 100.

If you decide not to, go to page 94.

Patagonian Lakes

- Brilliant blue lakes are scattered throughout the Patagonian Andes. An area known as the Lakes District includes about 20 large lakes, which were carved into the landscape during the last ice age. It's the greenest part of Patagonia, and is covered in temperate rainforests.

- General Carrera Lake in Patagonia is South America's deepest lake. It has a maximum depth of around 1,935 feet (590 m), and is roughly 124 miles (200 km) long, with an area of nearly 386 square miles (1,000 sq km). Beautiful marble cliffs, which have been sculpted into amazing shapes and caves, rise at the edges of the lake.

- Lake Viedma is fed by the Viedma Glacier, which flows into the lake. The spectacular ice sheet is 1.6 miles (2 km) wide at the western edge of the lake.

- Large Chilean flamingos are found in Patagonian lakes, especially the saltwater lakes. You might also see striking black-necked swans.

You spot a small herd of brown, slender, llama-like animals grazing not far away. They have very long necks, and you're close enough to see their huge brown eyes. They spot you and stampede away at top speed. You're sorry to see the beautiful creatures go. But they've left a thoughtful gift. Some of their fleecy hair is stuck to the dry, scrubby bushes dotted around. You collect some for insulation, in case you need to spend another night in the wilderness.

There's a cheeping noise close by and you spin around. Not far away, there's a big bird. It looks like an ostrich with dull gray-brown feathers, about three feet (1 m) tall. Running alongside the bird are three of its chicks.

The birds are obviously flightless. Maybe you could grab a chick and roast it. You are starting to feel weak with hunger by this point.

If you decide to chase one of the chicks, go to page 110.

If you decide to keep away from the birds and continue on your way, go to page 103.

Guanacos

- The animals you spotted are guanacos, which live in South America from southern Peru to Argentina and Chile. They can be found quite high up in the Andes Mountains—up to about 13,125 feet (4,000 m).

- Guanacos and vicuñas, and their close relatives are wild animals. Llamas and alpacas are domesticated or bred by humans from their wild relatives. All of these animals are related to camels.

- Guanacos have amazing coats and, like alpacas, they are bred for their fleece. Guanaco fleece is softer and more luxurious than alpaca fleece, but guanacos don't have as much fleece as alpacas.

- The animals live in groups of up to ten females with their young and a single male. There are also groups of young male guanacos, and these groups can be much larger. Males live together before they leave the herd to go in search of their own group of females.

A blue-white glacier stretches below you. In your bag there are some crampons, which are spiked overshoes that help you walk on ice and densely packed snow. You have them with you because you had planned to walk on a glacier as part of your trek. It might even have been this glacier, for all you know.

Glacier walking must be fun, if people regularly do it on treks. It looks smooth and easy to walk on. Maybe you should put on your crampons and walk on the glacier.

If you decide to walk on the glacier, go to page 66.

If you decide not to, go to page 102.

Glaciers

- A glacier is a river of ice. It moves slowly, though it usually doesn't look as though it's moving at all. But it is flowing like a river—in very slow motion.

- Some glaciers flow faster than others. The record goes to the Kutiah Glacier in Pakistan, which was clocked racing along at 367 feet (112 m) per day.

- A glacier begins to be formed when snow doesn't melt and more snow falls on top. Thick layers of snow are squashed into ice.

- There are different types of glaciers. Ice sheets are the largest type, covering thousands of square miles (kilometers). They are only found in Greenland and Antarctica. Ice shelves are ice sheets that float on the sea. There are various other types, too, including mountain glaciers.

- Ten per cent of Earth's surface is covered by glacial ice. Amazingly, glaciers store 75% of all the world's fresh water.

- The largest expanse of glacial ice outside the polar regions is found in southern Patagonia. There are 19 large glaciers, and the Campo de Hielo Sur (Southern Patagonian Ice Field) measures around 198 miles (320 km) from north to south.

You spend some time finding a good place to stop and make camp. You choose a site that's near a stream and on flat ground, but not in a valley, which might get flooded. It's nice and sheltered here, with woods nearby where you can find firewood and logs to make a shelter.

You've got time to spend, so you make a really good, sturdy shelter using lots of tree branches. You even find some fleecy hair stuck on some bushes, which you think has come from a guanaco (see page 95). You use it as insulation for your improvised sleeping bag. You build a fire pit and get a good fire burning (see page 87 for making a fire). Then you spell out SOS in enormous letters with rocks. You catch fish from the stream using a stick you have whittled into a spear. You've got plenty of water to drink.

You have to wait a week before you hear the reassuring sound of helicopter rotors in the distance. Your heart pounding, you make sure there's nothing covering your SOS letters, and you throw some green wood onto the fire to make smoke. The helicopter pilot sees you! You're soon taken to safety and reunited with your friends.

But you can't help wondering if it might have been an even better adventure to keep going.

The end.

You make your way around the edge of the lake. It's longer this way, and you have to negotiate large boulders by the lake side. But you don't like your chances on that ice. If it were to break and you fell in, you'd almost certainly die of hypothermia. You take your time, clambering over the boulders carefully so as not to risk getting injured.

Go to page 114.

You decide that your best chance of catching a fish will be to make a spear, then to lie on the bank and wait for a passing fish. The water is clear, and you don't have any bait for a hook anyway.

But as you approach the edge of the lake, you slip on a rock and plunge feet first into the water. The lake is fed by a glacier and it is so icy cold that it takes your breath away. You struggle out of the water. Only your feet and part of your legs are wet but, even so, it leaves you gasping from the shock of the cold water.

What should you do? Can you bear to take off your boots and clothes to dry them? Or is the thought of exposing your freezing legs to the elements too much to even consider?

If you decide to take off your clothes to get dry, go to page 82.

If you decide to keep walking and dry out that way, go to page 75.

Fishing

- The lake is full of fish. Among the fish that are good to eat are perch, which are native to this part of the world, as well as salmon and trout, which have been introduced here from North America.

- To hide from the fish, make sure your shadow doesn't fall on the surface of the water.

- If you don't have any luck spearing a fish with a sharpened stick, you could try making a trap. Use a plastic bottle with the top section cut off, turned around, and placed back inside the bottle so that the bottle top is facing into the bottom of the bottle. Fish can swim in through the narrow neck, but will find it very difficult to get out again.

- The biggest danger when fishing here is the cold water. As you've just found out, the waters of a glacier-fed lake are freezing cold.

The glacier looks easy to walk on, but you worry about falling into a crevasse or slipping, since you're not used to walking in your crampons. You decide instead to head down toward the lake.

Go to page 92.

As you continue on your way you notice that this side of the lake is frozen because it's in the shadow of a high mountain. On the other side of the lake, you catch sight of something moving fast. You strain your eyes to see. It's a hare, darting between the rocks as if it's running away from something. You spot the predator—an eagle, ready to swoop.

But as you move your eyes from the eagle back down to the ground, you notice something else. It looks as though there's a fence running along the other side of the lake. And on the other side of the fence, you can now make out some yellowish-white shapes. They're sheep! It must be a sheep farm—which means there must be people looking after the sheep, not too far away!

Although it's not too far across to the other side of the lake, to walk around the lake would take days—it's several times that distance and covered in boulders. The ice looks solid. Should you walk across the frozen lake, or go around the outside?

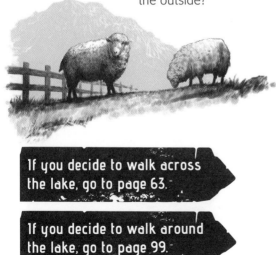

If you decide to walk across the lake, go to page 63.

If you decide to walk around the lake, go to page 99.

You decide to cook some of the stems and green leaves, which you hope will give you some much needed energy. You make a fire, boil a little water, add the plant, and cook it for a few minutes. It doesn't taste very nice, but you eat hungrily anyway.

You were right—you did indeed read about this plant in a book before you set off on your Andes trek. Unfortunately, it wasn't in the Edible Plant section. This plant is *Brugmansia sanguinea*, or blood-red angel's trumpet. It is sometimes eaten by people to fall into a trance and have visions as part of a religious ritual. You start to feel queasy and sit down. Your eyelids feel heavy . . . you fall into a strange waking sleep and dream you've turned into an alpaca. There's no one to look after you and keep you warm. Although the amount of the plant you've eaten wouldn't normally kill you, it keeps you in a trance long enough that you become too cold and develop hypothermia. You never wake up from your strange dream.

The end.

Angel's Trumpet

- Blood-red Angel's Trumpet is native to the Andes and grows in Bolivia, Colombia, Ecuador, Peru, and Chile.

- The plant can grow to be 16 feet (5 m) tall. It has thin, oval leaves and huge trumpet-shaped flowers around 8 inches (20 cm) long, that dangle down from the stems. The flowers can be pink to dark red. There's a very similar plant called the Golden Angel's Trumpet, which has fragrant white or yellow flowers.

- Some Andean people use the plant in rituals to communicate with the spirit world.

- The plant is also used by tribespeople as a medicine to clean wounds and to cure a wide variety of problems such as rheumatism, arthritis, sore throats and stomachaches.

Animals aren't known for their hygiene, and water holes can easily become contaminated. Unfortunately, that's what happened here. Boiling water will usually be enough to kill germs but, for some reason, you decided not to bother. Oh dear.

You carry on your way, but soon you start to feel feverish and sick. You vomit, but it doesn't make you feel any better. You try to struggle on, but keep having to stop because you now have diarrhea, too. You lie down. There's no one around to help you, and you don't have enough water and salt with you to replace the fluids you've lost. This is the end of the road for you.

The end.

Waterborne Diseases

There's a wide and horrible variety of diseases that can be transmitted in water. Here are some to look out for.

- Cholera – Spread by bacteria, cholera causes severe diarrhea. The disease can kill quickly if it's not treated.

- Dysentery – There are two types, one caused by bacteria and the other by parasites, but both cause vomiting and diarrhea. If the parasitic type of dysentery, called amoebic dysentery, isn't treated, it can kill you.

- Typhoid fever – Spread by an infected person's feces in drinking water, typhoid causes fever, sweating, and sometimes diarrhea. It can be fatal.

- There are a lot of others, such as parasites that live in your intestines, and viruses that can cause all sorts of horrible symptoms. In a survival situation, always boil water before you drink it.

Your foot slips as you scramble after the little animal. It's scurrying higher up among some boulders. You lose sight of the guinea pig, but you figure that you're bound to come across it, or one of its friends or relatives, if you keep going. On the other hand, maybe you should admit defeat. You're hungry, but are you hungry enough?

If you decide to stop looking for the guinea pig, go to page 113.

If you decide to keep climbing, go to page 68.

Your stomach rumbles. You haven't had a meal for such a long time, and you're desperately hungry. You might start to feel weak if you don't find something to eat soon.

You spot a plant you think you recognize—beautiful trumpet-shaped red flowers hang from a small tree. You are sure you saw the plant in a book about the Andes that you were reading before you started your trek. That probably means it's one of the plants that's safe to eat.

If you decide to eat some of the plant, go to page 104.

If you decide not to eat it, go to page 90.

You don't think the adult bird has spotted you. You creep slowly and carefully toward it and its chicks.

Suddenly the bird sees you. It throws out its flightless wings and screeches. You freeze. The bird is still agitated, and the chicks are cheeping frantically. Then the adult bird charges at you, moving incredibly fast. You take off, running as fast as your legs can carry you. In your panic, you trip over a boulder, bang your head, and knock yourself out. With no one around to look after you, you die.

The end.

Rheas

- These birds are called Darwin's rheas, or lesser rheas. There's also another type called the greater rhea.

- Adult Darwin's rheas can be up to three feet (1 m) tall. Amazingly, they can run at up to 37 miles (60 km) per hour.

- The birds are often found close to herds of guanacos or vicuñas, usually in groups of between five and 30 birds.

- The male rheas incubate the eggs, which is unusual for birds. The eggs take about 40 days to hatch, then the males care for the young bird for a few more months. Male rheas can be aggressive during the breeding season, and when incubating eggs or rearing young.

- The famous scientist Charles Darwin discovered Darwin's rheas. The group he was with shot one of the birds to eat. Darwin realized it was an unrecorded species, and salvaged part of it to study before it was all eaten!

As you round a rocky outcrop, you spot a bright blue lake below you. It's big and surrounded by boulders and scrubby grassland. There might be fish in the lake, and it would also be a good chance to fill up your water bottle.

You think it will take an hour or so to walk down to the lake. Should you change direction and go to the lake, or carry on the way you're going?

If you decide to walk toward the lake, go to page 92.

If you decide to keep going as you are, go to page 62.

You're still hungry, but you think you can keep your strength up enough to keep going. You know that water is far more important—you can survive for weeks without food. And, anyway, you're bound to be rescued soon.

You look at the sky hopefully, imagining a rescue helicopter or a plane, but all you can see are two condors against the blue sky.

You have to pick your way through large stones and boulders, which is tiring. But you keep going, telling yourself that everything will be all right.

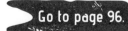 Go to page 96.

After what seems like a very long walk, you make it up to the fence.

In among the scattered sheep, you scan the horizon for signs of human life. You hear a faint shout and turn to see the most wonderful sight: two people on horseback, waving at you!

Before long, you're in a warm farmhouse, eating a hot meal, and trying out your Spanish. Soon, you're reunited with your friends.

Your mountain adventure is over, and you're safe at last!

The end.

The People of the Andes

People have lived in the Andes for thousands of years. The Yaghan people, for example, have lived in Tierra del Fuego for more than 10,000 years. Most of the indigenous people of South America eventually mixed with the settlers from Europe. There is one Yaghan woman who is the last Yaghan person alive. Most people speak Spanish now, but a few still speak the Yaghan language. Tierra del Fuego, which means "Land of Fire", was named because of the fires of the Yaghan people, which were spotted by the explorer Magellan on his expedition around the world.

Farther north, people live high up in the Andes Mountains. In the Bolivian and Peruvian Andes, the Incas ruled the largest empire in the Americas before the arrival of Europeans. Today, the highest capital city in the world is La Paz, in Bolivia, which is 11,942 feet (3,640 m) above sea level. Living at high altitudes is physically demanding because there is less oxygen, and people's bodies have had to adapt to living there.

The biggest group of native South American Indians are the Mapuche, most of whom live in Chile today. They fiercely resisted the Spanish conquerors from the 1500s to the 1700s. In the 1800s, the Chilean government settled the Mapuche people on areas of land called reservations.

Most of the people who live in the rural Andes live on farms and raise sheep, goats, llamas, and alpacas. There are also mines in the Andes, because of its deposits of coal, iron, silver, gold, tin, and copper. Yanacocha, in Peru, is one of the world's biggest gold mines.

In 1865, around 150 Welsh people landed in Patagonia and established Argentina's first Welsh colony. Today there are more than 1,000 Welsh-speakers in Patagonia.

Amazing Andes Animals

As well as the animals you've already met in this book (pumas, Patagonian foxes, guinea pigs, chinchillas, guanacos, South Andean deer, Andean condors, and rheas), the Andes are home to other incredible animals.

- Vizcachas are some of the world's cutest animals. They look like especially furry-gray rabbits with long tails, but they're actually related to chinchillas. They live in dry, desert environments high in the Andes, where they build vast networks of burrows. A different type of vizcacha lives in the plains of Argentina.

- Darwin's frogs are found in Chile and Argentina. They're brown or green with a long snout. They are unusual because the males incubate the eggs inside their mouths. After three weeks, fully formed froglets pop out. These frogs were first classified by Charles Darwin.

- Spectacled bears, the only bear in South America, live in the remote cloud forests of the Andes, as high up in the mountains as 14,100 feet (4,300 m). They're brown or black, usually with whiteish colored circles around their eyes, which is how they got their name. Male spectacled bears grow to be about 6 feet (1.8 m) and weigh about 330 pounds (150 km). They're mainly vegetarian, but they do eat meat sometimes.

- The yellow-tailed woolly monkey is found only in the Andes Mountains in Peru. It was thought to be extinct until it was rediscovered in 1974. Today it is still very rare.

Real-life Lost-in-the-Andes Stories

People really have become lost in the Andes, with horrifying consequences.

In 1972, a small plane carrying a Uruguayan rugby team from Argentina to Chile crashed in the Andes. The crash, plus an avalanche caused by the crash, left 26 of the 45 passengers and crew dead. The survivors had hardly any food, and the plane had crashed at 11,800 feet (3,597 m). They had a radio to listen to, but no means of signaling. After 11 days, they heard the news that the search for their plane had been given up. They resorted to eating some of the dead passengers whose bodies were preserved by the cold snow. Eventually, two of the survivors set off to find help and came across a remote farmhouse after a grueling ten-day trek. At the end of the ordeal, after 72 days on the mountain, there were 16 survivors left to be rescued.

In 1985, Joe Simpson and Simon Yates were climbing Siula Grande, a mountain in Peru. On the way back down the mountain, Simpson slipped and fell, breaking his leg. His friend was trying to lower him down the mountain when he was forced to cut the rope during a raging storm to save himself. Simpson fell 164 feet (50 m) but survived, and both he and Yates made it back to safety. Simpson wrote a book about their story, which was later made into a film called *Touching the Void*.

The Inca Empire

The Inca Empire spanned much of western South America across the Andes. These were tough people, living and working at an altitude much higher than most humans are used to. The Incas devised ingenious ways to adapt to the harsh Andes climate.

The Inca ruled from the mid-1400s until 1572, when the last stronghold fell to Spanish conquerors. In the late 1520s, the Spanish had begun to push into Inca territory, bringing with them smallpox, a disease that ultimately killed more than half the Inca population. Ultimately, the Spanish conquered the Incas, raiding their gold and silver, and wiping out their culture.

At its height, the Inca Empire included nearly 10 million people. About twenty different languages were spoken. Although they had no wheels, no iron, and no working animals, the Incas still managed to build a far-reaching military and political empire. They were known for their superior engineering, and many original Inca structures still exist today. In fact, the conquering Spanish felt that the Incas' road networks and cities were much better constructed than those back in Europe! But because the Incas had no written language, much of their history… remains a mystery.

Glossary

agile Able to move quickly and easily

altitude sickness Illness caused by the lack of oxygen when at a high altitude

avalanche Rapid fall of snow down a sloping surface

canopy Cover formed by a tree's branches

carabiner A metal ring and clip used for fastening ropes when climbing

carrion Dead animals

cerebral edema Buildup of fluid around the brain

chinchilla Type of rodent with a very soft, gray coat

condor Type of vulture; one of the largest flying birds

contaminated Unclean

crampons Plates with spikes that attach to your shoes so you can walk on ice

crevasse Deep, open crack in a glacier or ice sheet

destabilize Weaken

dysentery An infection causing diarrhea

edema Swelling in the body caused by buildup of fluid

extinct No longer existing

geyser Hot spring that sends spouts of hot water and steam into the air

glacier Large body of thick ice that is constantly moving

granite Grainy type of rock

guanaco Animal similar to a llama or an alpaca

hypothermia Having an abnormally low body temperature

incubate Keep eggs warm until they hatch, usually by sitting on them

kindling Small, dry twigs that will burn quickly and easily; used for lighting a fire

meltwater Water released by the melting of snow or ice

opportunistic Taking advantage of opportunities as they arise

parasite A creature that lives by attaching itself to and feeding on another creature

plain Broad expanse of flat land

precipice Very steep rock face or cliff

pulmonary edema Buildup of fluid around the lungs

puma Large, powerful wildcat

salvaged Saved

scavenge To feed on dead animals or plants

sheer Very steep

southern hemisphere Parts of Earth that lie south of the equator

tectonic plates Large slabs of rock that make up Earth's surface

temperate Having a mild climate

terrain Physical features of land

tinder Very dry material that is easy to set on fire

transceiver Device that gives out a signal to indicate where someone is

vicuña Animal similar to a llama or an alpaca

volcanic fissure Crack or vent through which lava erupts

Learning More

George, Jean Craighead. *My Side of the Mountain*. Puffin Modern Classics, 2001.

George, Jean Craighead. *Julie of the Wolves*. HarperCollins, 1997.

Mowat, Farley. *Lost in the Barrens*. Bantam Starfire, 1985.

Paulsen, Gary. *Hatchet*. Simon & Schuster Books for Young Readers, 2006.

Borgenicht, David, Joshua Piven, and Ben H. Winters. *The Worst Case Scenario Survival Handbook*. Chronicle Books, 2012.

Simpson, Joe. *Touching the Void: The True Story of One Man's Miraculous Survival*. HarperCollins Canada, 2004.

Tarshis, Lauren. *I Survived series*. Scholastic, 2010–2014.

Websites

Survival 101 (Backpacker Magazine)
www.backpacker.com/survival-101-how-to-survive-in-the-wilderness/skills/14407

A Kid's Wilderness Survival Primer Situation (Equipped to Survive Foundation)
www.equipped.org/kidprimr.htm

How to Build a Survival Shelter
www.natureskills.com/survival/primitive-shelter/

List of great books about survival (Indianapolis Public Library)
www.imcpl.org/kids/blog/?page_id=12516

Surviving: 7 Survival Rules
www.mounteverest.net/expguide/survivalrules.htm

Andes Mountains: Facts, Location & Quiz
www.education-portal.com/academy/lesson/andes-mountains-facts-location-quiz.html#lesson

Encyclopedia of Everything Mountains
www.mountainprofessor.com

Index

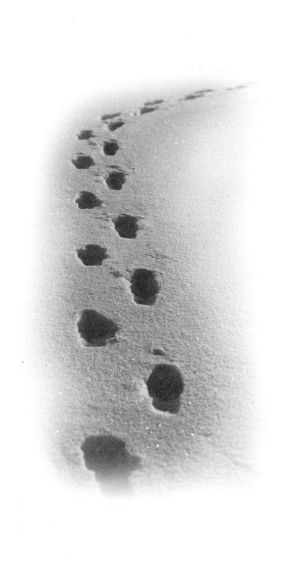